KB209484

나의
Korean Sonnet
英韓대역 14행시

六峰 정 동 희 지음
Jung, Dong-Hee

대학 영문학과 교재
강력 추천

行詩야 놀자
14 th

나의 코리언 소네트
English-Korean Bilingual
14th Acrostic Poem

한국행시문학회
도서출판한행문학

Preface My Korean Sonnet 시작하면서

My Korean Sonnet   나의 코리언 소네트
Yeah, the product of will and tenacity   의지와 끈기의 산물

Korean Sonnet is   코리언 소네트는
Only English-Korean 14 lines acrostic   리얼한 영한대역 14행시
Really the true magic of language   언어의 진정한 마술
Even writing only a handful of writer   소수의 작가만 쓰고 있다
And if the netizens find out it   네티즌들이 알게 되면
Now lots of people to train   트레이닝할 사람 많아요

Sonnet in the world a book   책 속의 소네트
Of course I think it's difficult   으레 어렵다 생각하지만
Not a fast like a rocket   로켓처럼 빠르진 않아도
Now if in my own way   나름대로 열심히 하면
English-Korean acrostic first in world   온 세상 처음인 영한행시
To the various sentences   다양한 문장이 반짝이네

- 2024. 8 / Jung, Dong-Hee

Contents 목차

- 서문 / Preface My Korean Sonnet / 002
- 목차 / Contents / 003
- 셰익스피어 소네트 / Shakespeare Sonnet / 006
- 코리언 소네트 / Korean Sonnet / 007
- 하나 뿐인 글 / Korean Language / 008
- 한글날 우리글 / Korean Language / 010
- 아름다운 푸른 눈동자 / Pretty Blue Eyes / 012
- 코로나 너! / Corona, You! / 014
- 바닷가의 예배당 / Chapel by the Sea / 016
- 흰 눈과 함께 / White Christmas / 018
- 다시 눈을 뜬다 / Energize Reopen / 020
- 완전한 세상 / A Whole New World / 022
- 10월의 숲 / October Forests / 024
- 대한민국 애국가 / National Anthem / 026
- 행시(行詩)는? / Acrostic Poem is / 028
- 홍하의 골짜기 / Red River Valley / 030
- 고마워요 / I'm fine thank you / 032
- 사랑은 시가 되고 / Writing True Win / 034
- 성경 말씀에 / The Bible Says / 036
- 365번 죽어야 해 / For Write to Poem / 038
- 그대의 맑은 미소 / Smile is / 040
- 바빌론 강 / River of Babylon / 042
- 고마워 한글 / Thank You Hangul / 044
- 평범하고 심플 / Plain and Simple / 046

❏ 1월 1일 / 1st January / 048
❏ 윤동주의 서시 / Yoon, Dong-Ju Poem / 050
❏ 아름다운 세상 / Beautiful Today / 052
❏ 03시 15분 전 / Quarter to Three / 054
❏ 존재의 이유 / You're the Reason / 056
❏ 가-나-다-라 / Ga-Na-Da-Ra / 058
❏ 내 사랑 내 곁에 / My love beside me / 060
❏ 꿈은 이루어진다 / Any Dream Will Do / 062
❏ 마음 담은 글 / Write with minds / 064
❏ 한 방에 끝 낸다 / One Shot One Kill / 066
❏ 성은 김이요(좌) / You're the Reason(L) / 068
❏ 성은 김이요(우) / You're the Reason(R) / 070
❏ 못 말린다 정동희 / Like Ray of Light / 072
❏ 나비부인 / Madam Butterfly / 074
❏ 참 좋은 벗 - 행시(行詩) / Acrostic / 076
❏ 나의 가을 단풍잎 / My Autumn Leaves / 078
❏ 지금 아니면 안 돼 / It is Now or Never / 080
❏ 안녕하세요? / How have you been? / 082
❏ 꽃들이 즐긴다 / Flowers Enjoying / 084
❏ 열애 / Passionate Love / 086

❏ 자신만 안다 / You Only it Known / 088
❏ 김정호의 작은 새 / A Small Bird / 090
❏ 탁구 / Ping-Pong / 092
❏ 六峰 정동희 73세 / It's me Seventies / 094
❏ 영어 회화 / English Conversation / 096
❏ 환영합니다 / Welcome to My World / 098
❏ 임영웅 / Star Young-Woong / 100
❏ 헌혈 불가 통보 / Blood Donations / 102
❏ 정신 나갔다, 병원 안 간다 / Fucks Your Minds / 104
❏ 웃어라 / Laugh on you want / 106
❏ 인생 70 즐겨라 / You Better Enjoy / 108
❏ 노후 처세 명심보감 12 / In my old age / 110
❏ 홀로 / Alone / 112
❏ 더 나은 매일 / Better Everyday / 114
❏ 롯데 엘리트 팀 / Lotte Elite Team / 116
❏ 당당하게 살자 / Best Life Keeper / 118
❏ 롯데손해보험 첫 급여 / My first payroll / 120
❏ 보험을 아시나요? / Did you know what? / 122
❏ 암은 사고처럼 온다 / Cancer Accident / 124
❏ 보험 없으면 위험한 인생 / Out of insurance / 126

Shakespeare Sonnet 셰익스피어 소네트

영한사전에 <u>14행시</u>로 번역되어 있는 <u>Sonnet(소네트)</u>는 유럽의 정형시 중 하나로, 단어 자체는 '작은 노래'를 의미한다. 이탈리아어식으로는 소네토(Sonetto)라고 한다.

소네트의 역사는 르네상스 시절 이탈리아의 단테 알리기에리가 그의 연인 베아트리체에게 보낸 서정시들로부터 유래했다. 이탈리아의 페트라르카가 이탈리아 소네트를 발전시켰고, 이를 영국의 토머스 와이엇이 이탈리아 소네트를 도입한 이래로 **셰익스피어**가 영시 형식으로 온전히 발전시키고 썼다.

영국식 소네트는 Shakespearian Sonnet(셰익스피어식 소네트)로도 불리며 네 줄씩 세 번이 나온 후 두 줄이 추가되는 quatrain + quatrain + quatrain + couplet 의 구조를 이룬다. **소네트의 형식**은 각 운을 엄격히 맞추며, <u>**영국식 소네트의 압운 형식은 abab + cdcd + efef + gg를 정확히 따른다**</u>. 셰익스피어식 소네트로 대표되는 영국식 소네트가 압운을 지키는데 있어서 이탈리아 소네트에 비해서 더 엄격하다. 국내에서 피천득 시인이 번역해서 출간한 '셰익스피어의 소네트'에는 셰익스피어 소네트 154편이 들어있다. 대표적인 소네트 작가로는 프란체스코 페트라르카, 윌리엄 셰익스피어, 존 밀턴, 윌리엄 워즈워스 등이 있으며 자료로도 찾아볼 수 있다.

Korean Sonnet 코리언 소네트(한글 소네트)

13세기~16세기 때부터 전래된 유럽의 **셰익스피어 소네트가 14行으로 이루어졌으며**, 이에 대하여 **英韓 대역 14행시를 Korean Sonnet(한글 소네트)로 명명하기로 한다**.

정확한 통계는 없으나 대략 3,000여명으로 추산되는 전국의 행시인들과 해외동포 행시인들이 계시지만, 2001년부터 지금까지 24년째, 자유시나 시조, 수필, 소설 등 다른 장르는 전혀 쓰지 않고 행시만 쓰고 있으며, 특히 2010년부터 영어도 행시가 되면서 동시에 한글도 행시가 되는 **英韓 대역 행시를 쓰고 있는, 현재로서는 유일한 행시인인 필자**가 그 동안 가나다라 14행시와, 가나다라가 아닌 일반 14행시 중에서 英韓대역으로 쓴 약 200편 중에서 약 60편을 선별하여 책으로 낸다.

물론 향후 더 많은 행시인들이 英韓 대역 행시에 도전하셔서 붐이 일어나길 간절히 바라고 있으며, 조언을 아끼지 않는다. 이 길이 결코 어렵지는 않다고 보는 이유가 1) 영어전공자도 아니며 2) 미국 유학파도 아니고 3) 올해 나이 일흔 넷에 이렇게 쓰고 있는데, 더 젊고 유능하신 행시인들의 도전이 요망된다. **필자가 쓰는 영어행시는 가급적 쉬운 단어만 골랐고 문장도 길지 않게 쓰고 있어서 이 책도 이해가 쉬울 것으로 본다**.

Korean Language

King Se-jong who is highest person

Of course this letters made by him

Really so many person can to learn

Eventually after the live work

At that time finished of the day

Not delay immediately proclaim it

Learn easy for the learning people

Any one use it very well

Nowadays it's good one of proud

Good letter differs from other

Use Kakao system on nowadays

Always easy to typing

Good effect for ripple to everyone

Especially it's the only best letter

- Korean Sonnet #003 / 2020. 10. 9

하나 뿐인 글

가장 높은 님
나랏님이 만든 글
다 알 수 있게
라이브 작업 끝에
마침표 찍고
바로 선포 하셨지

사람들 쉽게 배워
아무나 쓰고
자랑해도 될 만한
차이 나는 글
카카오 쓰는 요즘
타이핑 쉽고
파급효과도 좋은
하나 뿐인 글

Korean Language

Know the Korean language and then
Of course I'm write line poem with English
Really I'm happy day by day
Each letters are own language so
Amazing pride makes me excited
Now these articles pretty shine

Language meaning is happiness
Always achieve it anyway
Noble work get recognized
Generally leading it quietly
Usually live with line poems
All the time day and day
Good as much as great
Every time is all beautiful

- Korean Sonnet #004 / 2020. 10. 9

한글날 우리 글

한글을 알고

글로 행시를 쓴다

날로 기쁘다

우리 글이라

리얼한 자긍심에

글이 빛난다

행복의 의미

시인이 일궈내고

인정 받으며

은근히 앞장 선다

행시에 묻혀 사는

복된 나날이

하늘 만큼 땅 만큼

다 아름답다

Pretty Blue Eyes

Pretty of you now
Really curious where are you from
Eyes so clear always
Thou are so beautiful quietly
The moment of eye contact
You know the energy rises

But without the reason
Looking and keep going into you
Usually feeling of excitement
Energy is good caused by you

Eyes closed for a moment
You know I try to calm down
Eventually in the presence of you
So open my eyes again

- Korean Sonnet #005 / 2021. 2. 26

아름다운 푸른 눈동자

그대는 지금
대체 어디서 왔나
맑은 눈동자
은은한 자태
눈이 마주친 순간
에너지 불끈

나도 모르게
자꾸만 빨려 들고
신명 나는 느낌과
이 좋은 기분

잠시 눈 감고
겨우 진정해 봐도
든직한 그 모습에
다시 눈 뜬다

Corona, You!

Go! Go out!

However don't you go out?

In these day just looking at it

Just gonna you sit down forever

Korean Air Line ticket I'll give you

Let's talk what I really want

May listen you're gentleman

Notice! You leave before fall

Only I'll watch you about it

Proper procedure you do it

Quiet if it works well, I'll drink

Really goodbye to star

So I want to shout

Then I'll smile fu-ha-ha

- Korean Sonnet #006 / 2021. 3. 7

코로나 너!

가라 **가**

안 나가**나**

눈치만 보**다**

영 주저 앉을**라**

비행기 티켓 주**마**

내가 진정 원하는 **바**

내 말 잘 들으면 넌 신**사**

가을 전 떠나는 게 좋**아**

잘 하는지 지켜 보**자**

제대로 하는 절**차**

잘 되면 한잔 **카**

잘 가라 스**타**

외치고 **파**

푸하**하**

Chapel by the Sea

Christ Jesus who is son of God
He's here as my savior
Always I'm living with him
Perhaps I haven't met him but
Every time I'm seeing him
Lot of drizzle in there

Being while in my whole life
You know throw away all my doubts

The one who can I see
However you're in dotcom too
Eventually you're my close friend

Sometimes when I were outside of church
Even I was wondering
All the time you hold me confidently

- Korean Sonnet #008 / 2021. 10. 8

바닷가의 예배당

하나님 아들 예수
나의 구주로 오신
님과 더불어 사네
만나보지 못해도
나는 만나고 있네
는개비 맞으면서

나 일생 사는 동안
의심 모두 버리고

바라볼 수 있는 님
닷컴 속에도 계신
가장 가까운 내 님

예배당 바깥에서
배회하는 이 몸을
당차게 붙드시네

White Christmas

With I rolling in the white snow

However I did without a glance

It with excessive passion

To shouting loudly

Even abandon the fear

Courage only I have

However in the rough world

Really I cross a whirlpool fast

In the harmony and unity

So many answer do we need

Then I did it all right

Mainly rolling with the acrostic

Always I enjoyed it like crush

So with an erotic sensation

- Korean Sonnet #010 / 2021. 12. 25

흰 눈과 함께

흰 눈 속에 뒹굴며
눈길도 주지 않고
과한 열정과 함께
함성을 지르면서
께름칙함 버리고

용기 하나만 갖고
서슬 시퍼런 세상
와류도 성큼 건너
화합과 단결 속에
해답이 필요할 때
의례 나는 해냈다
몸소 뒹굴던 행시
짓누르듯 즐겼다
에로틱한 감으로

Energize reopen

Energy has been greatly reduced

Now not cool moving my body

Everything is done I think

Really at the age of mine

Generally and so do my friends

In this time as it is

Zero to return is impossible but

Every time if I could grab it

Run again I want to it

Every day let's restart

Of course eye is dim sighted now

Push off the inconvenience

Even if all night with eyes open

Now I'm running again

- Korean Sonnet #013 / 2022. 5. 23

다시 눈을 뜬다

에너지도 크게 줄고
돌아가는 게 심상찮아
다 된 것 같다

지금 내 나이에
친구들도 다 그렇단다

그 자리에 그대로
리턴은 안 되겠지만
움켜잡을 수만 있다면

다시 달리고 싶다
시작을 다시 하자

눈이야 침침하지만
을밋함은 털어버리겠다
뜬눈으로 밤을 샐지라도
다시 뛴다 지금

A Whole New World

As this whole life

What a my full fledged dream
Hugging all of them
Of course day by day
Live with gratitude
Even rough world

New light of tomorrow and
Every day with romance
We enjoy the luck

We have meet is
Only inevitable phenomenon
Really it without stand for others
Lots of meaningful within the world
Definitely open my imagination

- Korean Sonnet #014 / 2022. 5. 24

완전한 세상

이 한 생 살며

완전한 내 꿈
전부 껴안고
하루 하루를
고맙게 산다
도도한 세상

새로운 빛과
로망을 안고
운을 즐긴다

우리들 만남
리얼한 필연
들러리 없는
세상 속에서
상상 펼친다

October Forests

On my optimistic life

Colorful leaves become thick

The autumn wind blows at times

Often troubled with others

Be while a heart of excitement

Eventually swallows in folds

Really that also my destiny

Finally I have a little left

Over the trace of righteous life

Red my autumn is ripe

Even poorly my day

Seeing at the round sky

Take draw on my canvas

So I remembered the summer

- Korean Sonnet #018 / 2022. 10. 1

10월의 숲

낙관적 삶에
엽색은 짙어가고
이따금 추풍
더러는 부대끼고
욱 하는 심정
고이 접어 삼킨다
운명이러니

나머지 남은
의로운 흔적 위로
가을은 익고
을밋한 날도
동그란 하늘 보며
화폭 채운다
여름을 떠올리며

National Anthem

Now the best position in the East and West

Actually recognized it from abroad

There is an old fact certainly

It's such a really great country

Of course don't know if it's a 100 points

Nowadays we've a first class skills

As you know we're not an oil producer but

Let me think why does it a unique being

Always as if I'd finally waited

National character should be faster like Lecaf

The high speed is always our strong point

Holy mountain of Paekdu does not dry up

East Sea also inexhaustible waters

Mainly our long history speaks for itself

- Korean Sonnet #027 / 2023. 4. 3

대한민국 애국가

동서양에서 최고의 지위

해외에서도 알아준다

물론 오래된 팩트라

과연 대단한 나라이다

백 점짜리는 아니겠지만

두 번째 아닌 첫 번째 솜씨도 있다

산유국도 아니면서

이 분야에 독보적인지 생각해 본다

마침내 기다렸다는 듯이 항상

르까프처럼 **빨리빨리** 하는 국민성

고속처리는 언제나 우리 강점이다

닳아 없어지지 않는 거룩한 백두산

도저히 마르지 않는 동해 바닷물

록록치 않은 우리 역사가 말해준다

Acrostic Poem is

Always by pre-rhymed
Could be we've rehearse
Really we have to rhyme tidied
Only write one line at a time
Start well must be decided rhyme
They will must not fall by mistake
It must write as our wish
Case by case it has to fit right

Probably it fits well anyway
Only it'll hard if don't write right
Eventually if lazy, could be fail
Maybe we can meet good rhyme

It dally away we can finished it
So don't know a poem until try it

- Korean Sonnet #029 / 2023. 4. 9

행시 (行詩)는?

미리 운을 정하고
리허설을 하기도 한다

정돈된 운에 잘 맞추고
한번에 한 줄씩 써나간다

운은 시작부터 잘 정해야 하며
으라차 실수로 무너지지 않아야 하고
로망 대로 써야 한다

딱딱 경우에 따라 잘 맞아야 하고
딱 맞도록 어차피 맞춘다

맞지 않게 쓰면 물론 힘이 들고
게으르면 결국 실패한다

쓰다 보면 좋은 운을 만날 수도 있고
는적거리다가 완성할 수도 있다

시는 써보기 전에는 모른다

Red River Valley

Red day, the valley is open with pleasure
Every time the white and blue stars lots spill
During stand up and body burns hot

Really man has exciting with a woman
In the moment of climax with dragon exhale
Very quickly breathing for a cheery tomorrow
Evening's going to be full anyway
Really time goes and It can't come back

Value of golden time does can come back?
A new body with a new energy If I have
Lots of day can I enjoy a new feeling?
Lots of imagined and wished for it
Even have a not good and can't expect more
You know I'm too old and don't have time

- Korean Sonnet #039 / 2023. 5. 5

홍하의 골짜기

홍박사 오신날도 흔쾌히 열린계곡
하얀별 파란별이 무수히 쏟아지고
의연히 일어선몸 뜨겁게 타오르니

골풀무 옹알이에 살송곳 물만난듯
짜르르 통한순간 용털임 쏟아내고
기운찬 새날위해 빠르게 숨고른다

다가올 저녁놀은 어차피 차올랐고
시간은 하염없이 흐르고 못오는데
금보다 귀한시간 다시금 올수있나

만약에 새기운에 새몸을 가진다면
날마다 새기분을 즐길수 있는건가
수없이 상상하고 염원을 해보지만

있는것 별일없고 새것은 기대난망
나이도 넘어섰고 세월도 짬이없네

I'm fine thank you

I search for this, shouldn't I have?
Maybe no ward it begins with 'chan'

Fuck you! there's a word missing
It's really crazy
Now well actually
Even I didn't start it with reluctantly

There been writing so many things
However I've seen this happen
Always I get really embarrassed
Now there's a crazy rhyme that says
Key point just think it and thank you

Yeah, what's big deal about living?
Of course if I live until the sun sets
Usually is this the end of my life

- Korean Sonnet #040 / 2023. 5. 6

고마워요

괜히 이걸 찾아봤나?
찮'으로 시작하는 단어는 없나 봐
아 글쎄 없는 단어도 있네요
요지경이야 정말

고게 사실은
마지못해 시작한 일은 아닌데
워낙 여러 글을 쓰다 보니
요런 경우도 있네요

정말 당황스러울 때도 많고
말도 안 되는 운(韻)도 있어요

감사해야지요 핵심만 생각합니다
사는 게 별 게 있나요?
해가 다 질 때까지 살다 보면
요정도로 살다가 끝나겠지요

Writing True Win

What is the love no**w**?

Rendezvous is the love**r**?

It's wrong subtly, sem**i**~

Try to write the poem, does i**t**?

I wanna that you'd better the acrostic min**i**

Not too long is good choose**n**

Go to write with agonize over lon**g**

True inner endurance i**t**

Right direction of life nea**r**

Usually can't bitten back to yo**u**

Every light burning at light speed tru**e**

Way to go like this slo**w**

I'm not pretending max**i**

Now look to the next generatio**n**

- Korean Sonnet #043 / 2023. 5. 7

사랑은 시가 되고

사랑이 무엇이라 생각하사?
랑데부가 연인이라고랑?
은연중 틀리셨노라 뜻은

시를 쓰고 있느뇨, 시?
가급적 행시를 원하시는가?
되도록 짧게 쓰시되
고심해서 쓰시고

내면의 참 인내
삶의 방향 제대로 잡은 삶
도로 물릴 수 없어도

빛의 속도로 매번 타오른 빛
이대로 이 길로 간다 한가로이
난 척 하지 않는 난
다음 세대를 바라본다

The Bible Says it

There's always plenty
Honorable at all times
Even if it's done according to pray

By the way I'll not be boast
It'll just in case
Bad situation, even if rival succeeds
Let see I don't be offended
Eventually think of it as a challenge

So I'll do my best every day
At last time to laugh
You'd better always with gratitude
Spirit of love also better

In an infinite spirit of service
Thus I'll wait for the next round

- Korean Sonnet #049 / 2023. 5. 18

성경 말씀에

항상 넉넉하고
상시 명예롭고

기도대로 될지라도
뻐기지 않으리라
하다 못해
라이벌이 성공을 해도

기분 나쁘게 생각 않고
도전의 기회로 여기고
하루 하루 정진하겠다
라스트에 웃기 위해서

감사한 마음으로
사랑의 정신으로
하염없는 봉사정신으로
라운드를 기다리리라

For Write to Poem

First
Of course I was born
Really in 1951

What a maniac for acrostic poem
Really in broad daylight
It 6 line, 8 line acrostic poem
To write 14 line too
Even at night when everyone's asleep

Then even don't stop
Of course write like lightning

Probably writing poetry to death
Only it's truly amazing but
Every no one scolding me
Maybe it's too much

- Korean Sonnet #057 / 2023. 6. 29

365번 죽어야 해

일단
년식은
에누리 없이 51년식

삼행시 매니아다
백주 대낮에도
육행시 팔행시
십사행시도 쓰고
다 잠든 밤중에도
셧다가 가는 법도 없이
번개같이 행시만 쓴다

죽도록 행시만 쓰니
어지간히 대단하다만
야단 치는 사람도 없고
해도 너무 하는 것 같다

Smile is

So do I just have to take off mask?
Maybe I'm gonna take it off first, but
It doesn't work out, even if I try again
Last in time, it will be easy
Eventually I expect a little bit

It's immature to pray right away
So very worried about it in all thing

So take it off mask, you fool
Make it welll lets do it our own
If doesn't do what you want, kick him
Last moment, if goes well it's king card
Even subtly comfortable with typing

I want to put it off until get power
Surely I want to relax all day, wow!

- Korean Sonnet #061 / 2023. 8. 4

그대의 맑은 미소

가면그것만벗으면되는가

나부터대충벗어보려하나

다시해도의도대로안된다

라스트에해맑게잘되리라

마지막까지좀은기대하마

바로기도해봐도미숙한바

사실내가걱정이많소매사

아예그걸벗겨라이사람아

자진해대충알아서잘하자

차라리내의중안따르면차

카드풀려해맑게되면킹카

타이핑이되니은근히편타

파워생길때까지미루고파

하루왼종일쉬고싶소하하

River of Babylon

Really even if it looks easy
It's so difficult
Very rewarding writings
Everybody's understanding and
Really need your help

Or directly
Finally with real interest

Basically easily from the beginning
Anyway if you start over now
Before didn't have it, you feel like it
You know implicitly improve it will
Lots of read and
Of course you'd better make a move
Now poetry will become your friend

- Korean Sonnet #064 / 2023. 8. 14

바빌론 강

쉬워 보여도
워낙 어렵고
보람된 글이다
여러분들의 이해와
도움이 필요하다

그 리고 직접
리얼한 관심 가지고

쉽게 기초부터
지금 새로 시작하면
않던 기분도 생기고
은연 중에 나아진다
글을 많이 읽고 또
行동에 옮겨보면
詩가 친구가 된다

Thank You Hangul

Too easy Korean language
Honorable elegant writings
Always why don't you learn
Now it's international sense
Knock! Come on! Hurry up!

You'd better good start now
Of course it's clean so much
Unbelievably knack is easy

However let's start together
Anyway if we learn together
Nothing is difficulty like this
Good to learn at any times
Usually this language is best
Let's show this off all times

- Korean Sonnet #068 / 2023. 10. 9

고마워 한글

Global Hangul Campaign

쉬운 한국어
운치 있는 글
한번 배워 봐
국제적 감각
어서 두드려

좋은 스타트
아주 깔끔해
요령도 쉬워

다 함께 시작
같이 배우면
이처럼 쉬워
배우기 좋은
우리 글 최고
자랑해 보자

지구촌 한글 캠페인

Thankyouhangul.com

Plain and Simple

Plain and simple English-Korean acrostic
Lovely and usual sentences
Actually it's not hard to write one a day
If you've immune about it, write it routinely
Now hurry up write today's acrostic

And choose the word as easy as possible
Non-negative, and mild expression
Directly once you read it, the meaning comes

Such as the English-Korean dictionary and
In fact, don't need a English dictionary
Mostly as simple word is good word
Probably it also desirable
Let's begin if you're interested it
Everyone can only get it if you start

- Korean Sonnet #079 / 2023. 12. 30

평범하고 심플

평범하고 단순한 영한대역 행시
범상하면서 사랑스러운 문장들
하루 하나씩 쓰는 건 어렵지 않고
면역 생기면 일상적으로 씁니다
서둘러 오늘 몫 행시를 써봐야지

단어는 가급적 쉬운 걸로 고르고
순한 표현, 부정적이지 않은 표현
한번 읽으면 의미가 전달돼 오는

영한 사전 같은 것이나
한영사전 굳이 찾지 않아도 되는
대체로 심플한 단어가 좋고
역시 바람직합니다
행여 구미가 당기면 시작 하세요
시작해야만 얻을 수 있습니다

1st January

Anyway who can stop changing year

Busy schedule in my own way

Could be the others did, too

Definitely last time is just one second

Eventually because it's ding last time

Fast changed the date immediately

Get out wanted follow rabbit actually

However I don't think it's gonna work

I sat back down

Just I thought calmly

K-acrostics with charisma is needed

Let me got it the target

Mostly with the blue lights on

Now begin to write one by one

- Korean Sonnet #081 / 2024. 1. 1

1월 1일

가는 해를 누가 말리나

나름대로 바빴지만

다른 사람들도 그랬을 거야

라스트 시간 딱 1초

마지막 땡 하니까 결국

바로 빠르게 해가 바뀌더군

사실 토끼 따라가고 싶었지만

아무래도 아니 될 것 같아서

자리에 도로 앉았어요

차분하게 생각했지요

카리스마 K-행시가 좋겠다

타겟을 정했으니

파란 불 켜고

하나씩 쓰기 시작합니다

Yoon, Dong-Ju Poem

Yeah, stars are blowing in the wind tonight

Of course it's like the wind always blows

Only the night sky is so beautiful

Now I want to write an essay

Down-coming like a thief

Of course the stars are beautiful

Now, as brushes my forehead

Good, the wind is

Joy of surge with these

Usually I want to put it in an essay

Put it with an unspoken writing

On a little emotion, I'd like to have

Even I wanted to write a good letter

Make focus again I want

- Korean Sonnet #082 / 2024. 1. 4

윤동주의 서시

오늘밤 별이 바람에 스친다

늘 불던 바람 같지만

밤 하늘이 너무 고와서

에세이 한 편을 쓰고 싶다

도둑 같이 내려온

별빛도 아름답고

이마에 스치듯 지나는

바람이 좋다

람실거리는 이 기쁨

에세이에 늘 담고 싶어서

스스럼 없는 글로 남기고

치기 어린 약간의 감정으로

운 좋은 글을 쓰기 원해서

다시 한번 집중해 본다

Beautiful Today

Brightest today, I'm young today

Even in pretty world, I'm pretty today

Actually we live in proud, proud today

Useful greatest day, I'm happy today

Today living best day ever, lucky today

If the world just collaps, I standing

Full busy day also, write today too

Usually all person I meet, precious them

Let's don't flatter myself, be cautious

Today even if a lot of hard work, I'm fine

Only no matter anyone says, I'll hold it in

Definitely eat with good friends, I pay

Actually without much talk, listen today

You collect these works, to publish book

- Korean Sonnet #083 / 2024. 1. 8

아름다운 세상

이 날은 최고로 밝은 날, 오늘은 젊어
아름다운 세상을 만나, 오늘은 예뻐
름름하게 살고 있지요, 당당한 오늘
다시 없는 최고의 오늘, 오늘 행복해
운 좋게 오늘을 보낸다, 오늘은 행운
세상이 혹시 무너져도, 오늘은 선다
상당히 바쁜 일 많아도, 오늘도 쓴다
만나는 모든 사람들을, 소중히 여겨
나 혼자만 잘난 척 않고, 오늘은 신중

너무 힘든 일이 많아도, 오늘은 거뜬
무슨 소리를 누가 하든, 오늘은 참아
좋은 님들과 밥 먹을 때, 오늘은 쏜다
아무 때나 떠들지 않고, 오늘은 듣자
요런 작품 착착 모아서, 책 발간 해요

Quarter To Three

Quietly I'm writing all night
Up to mind about the new writing
Actually keep writing it
Really writing has become my hobby
This has become a favorite pastime but
Even because my meager skill
Really I need more needs sometimes

Three o'clock already
Of course don't have energy to use but

The acrostic is so good among the poems
However while writing without a rest
Really into English-Korean bilingual acrostic
Even I'm write without knowing the world
Enjoy my time

- Korean Sonnet #086 / 2024. 1. 11

03시 15분 전

밤새 조용히 글을 쓴다
새 글에 대한 시상이 떠올라
글을 계속 쓰게 된다
쓰는 게 나의 취미가 됐다
다시 없는 취미지만
보잘것없는 솜씨에
니즈가 가끔은 더 필요하다

벌써 시간이 세시나 되어
써버릴 에너지도 딸리지만

시 중에서 行詩가 너무 좋아서
간단없이 쓰는 가운데
이제는 英韓대역 행시에 빠져
세상 모르고 쓰면서
시간을 즐기고 있다

You're the Reason

You're the reason that I live
Order from the God
Under the myself subtly
Really captivated all of me
Even implausible being

The reasons to live
However no one can stop you
Even implausible being

Really without any time to lose
Even without knowing why
Actually I'm getting sucked in
So it's my current life
Of course right now my life is
Now it's rolling like this

- Korean Sonnet #089 / 2024. 1. 21

존재의 이유

당신은 내가 살아가는
신이 주신 이유입니다
은연중 내 속에 스며들어

내 전부를 사로잡은
가당치 못할 존재

살아가는 이유
아무도 못 말릴
가당치 못할 존재
는적댈 새도 없이

이유도 모른 채
유유히 빨려 듭니다
이제는 제 생활이 됐고
지금은 제 인생이
요런 모습으로 굴러갑니다

Ga-Na-Da-Ra

Always I'm writing Ga-na-da

Basically I'm on my own

Could be at night everyone's asleep

Definitely looking for alphabet Ra

Even wander about wildly

From Korean alphabet Ba

Guard by dictionary, if not

However it's puzzling

It's after alphabet Ja also

Just traffic at alphabet Cha

Ka also stop there

Lots burning heart

Maybe if stop the alphabet Pa too

Now I've been hard long day

- Korean Sonnet #091 / 2024. 1. 26

가-나-다-라

가나다 쓰며

나홀로 끙끙

다 잠든 밤에

라字 찾느라

마구 설치네

바字 부터는

사전 안보면

아리까리 해

자字 다음에

차字 막히고

카字 못맞춰

타는 속마음

파字 또막혀

하루 힘드네

가나다 行詩

행시야놀자 시리즈 ④ / 鄭東熙

가나다 쓰며
나홀로 끙끙
다 잠든 밤에
라字 찾느라
마구 설치네
바字 부터는
사전 안보면
아리까리 해
자字 다음에
차字 막히고
카字 못맞춰
타는 속마음
파字 또막혀
하루 힘드네

010-6309-2050

My love beside me

My age is 74 now
You know so far so good but

Later I'm older
On many parts when I'm not well
Very bad become about some parts
Even can't touch more the keyboard

Because of my body doesn't work
Even can't write like this writing
So I can't take care of myself
Is the my mind intact?
Dear acrostic that enjoyed in high spirits
English-Korean bilingual acrostic like this

Many books as possible I'll keep
Eventually I'll keep it in the book case

- Korean Sonnet #092 / 2024. 1. 28

내 사랑 내 곁에

나 지금 일흔 넷
이제까지는 괜찮지만

더 나이 먹은 뒤에
들쭉날쭉 몸이 안 좋아서
어디가 매우 나빠지고
서서히 키보드도 못 치면

몸이 말을 안 들으니
이런 글도 못 쓸 것이고
나 스스로 못 챙기니
정신인들 온전할까?
신명 날 때 즐기던 행시
이런 영한대역 행시

가급적 책으로 많이 남겨
도서함에 잘 보관해야지

Any Dream Will Do

Any dream will do
Now will be do like imagined
You'd better put your energy into it

Definitely no matter how you go
Really if you have the guts
Even dreams can come true
Actually even without being best man
Maybe it's implicitly reachable

What a dream I want to achieve
If I know the root well
Let'll get there somehow
Lets don't need any questions

Directly you want to go straight there
Of course you have to be ambitious

- Korean Sonnet #096 / 2024. 2. 9

꿈은 이루어진다

세상에 모든 꿈들은
상상대로 이루어질 거야
에너지를 여기에 쏟아봐요

모로 가더라도
든든한 배짱만 있으면
꿈은 이룰 수 있고
들러리 서지 않고도
은연중 도달이 가능해요

이루고 싶은 꿈은
루트만 잘 안다면
어떻게든 가보자고요
질문은 필요 없어요

거기에 바로 가고 싶다면
야망은 당연히 있어야지요

Write with minds

Writing and I'm living
Really when I want to write it
It takes no matter how many nights
To ignoring arithmetic
Even write with boldly

Without eating
I don't fall down still now
To the point of not death I'm writing
Hardship is behind me

Mostly even if I don't sleep
I'm not too tired and
Never sick I think
Definitely maybe it's become a habit
So I can't fix it now

- Korean Sonnet #101 / 2024. 3. 6

마음 담은 글

글 쓰며 산다
쓰고 싶을 때는
며칠 밤이건
산수 셈법 무시하고
다부지게 쓴다

먹지 않고
지금까지도 뻗지
않을 정도로 쓴다
고생은 뒷전이다

자지 않아도
지치지도 아프지도
않는 것 같다
아마 습관이 돼서
도저히 못 고친다

One Shot One Kill

One shot one kill
Net translated Korean-English same time
Energy is some required to this work

Some time needed it takes but
However not exactly same if work it
Only translate uses internet translator
To see if it's right compare each other

Only rhyme Korean and English both
Now I check it if net translate wrong
Easy paraphrase often I did in short

Kill time is about 1 hour to end a each
I throw away because I can't end it
Let's start with mind to finish it own
Let's do it I never have chance again

- Korean Sonnet #103 / 2024. 3. 7

한 방에 끝낸다

한번에 시작, 한번에 마친다
번역과 영역을 거의 동시에
에너지가 좀 필요한 작업이다

시간은 어느 정도 걸리지만
작업해 보면 꼭 그렇지도 않다
해석은 인터넷 번역기를 이용
서로 비교하면서 맞는지 확인

한글, 영문, 동시에 운을 넣고
번역기가 오판하는지 살핀다
에둘러 말하자면 의역도 한다

끝마치는데 대략 1작품 1시간
마치지 못해 버리는 글도 있다
친히 끝낼 각오로 시작한다
다시 없는 기회로 여기고 한다

You're the Reason(L)

You know her full name is
Of course I can't tell you
Usually don't want to leak
Really I've never forgotten it
Even I remember this

This name I will now
However if I make it clear, so
Every one find out who is she

Really do disrespect me or
Etiquette, if you say 'No etiquette'
All styles become wrinkle
So I'm going to shut up about this
Only with my headed down
Now and then I'll just go like this

- Korean Sonnet #104 / 2024. 3. 8

성은 김이요(좌)

성과 이름은
은근히 못 밝힙니다
김 새면 안 되잖아요
이제까지 잊지 못하고
요렇게 기억합니다

이름을 제가 지금
름름하게 밝혀버리면
은연 중에 누군지 알고

디스를 하거나
에티켓 어쩌고 하면
스타일 다 구겨지니까
라스트 무덤까지
고개 숙인 채
요렇게 갑니다

You're the Reason(R)

of course I know her name anyway

but right now it's no

if open it leak all as know you

my requirements call for

has it been delivered are

without a thought

don't open the name and touch

now that we're disconnected line

a word to add clear

by any chance to where

stress we get when open idea

can't handle it's serious

must shut my mouth so

I just go, we don't known

- Korean Sonnet #105 / 2024. 3. 9

성은 김이요(우)

물론 압니다 그녀의 성
그러나 지금은
밝히면 다 새지요 김
제 뜻이
명확히 전달 되셨나요

아무 생각 없이
밝힐 수 없는 이름
특히 연락이 끊긴 지금은

확실히 덧붙일 한 마디
혹시라도 어디에
알려질 때 받을 스트레스
감당이 불감당이라
입 꾹 닫고
그냥 지나 가자고요

Ray of Light

Life, an unstoppable my life
It's no use trying to stop me
Knocked lynched if
Even can go to next generation

Really I love acrostic poem
Actually I've no fixed time
You know I'm fall in romance

Of course it's fun to live
For no time to lose I have

Lot of compassion I have, so
I'm join with the club members
Going always to flirt with them
High value writing a life acrostics
Thou enjoy life all the time

- Korean Sonnet #107 / 2024. 3. 12

못 말린다 정동희

못 말리는 인생
말려도 소용없다
린치라도 당하면
다음 세대 가면 돼

행시가 좋아
시도 때도 없지만
로망에 빠져

사는 재미 쏠쏠해
는적댈 새도 없어

정은 많아서
동호인들 어울려
희희덕대고
인생 행시 쓰면서
생을 즐긴다

Madam Butterfly

Melted into my life, the acrostic
Anyway it become my life without a doubt
Day by day I write something I like
Actually my daily life by enjoy the fun
Mostly I getting a lot of energy

Before sunrise the morning sit on computer
Usually all day since I don't go to work
Therefore I have no days or nights
Though I don't have to be wary of others
Everything I'm doing it on my own way
Really I draining all the energy I've left
Finally it's going without a moments delay
Lots of my written articles so far, but
You know feel like a lesser human being

- Korean Sonnet #116 / 2024. 4. 9

나비부인

나의 인생에 녹아든, 행시
의심의 여지 없이 내 삶이 되었다
마음에 드는 작품 매일 쓰면서
음풍농월을 일삼는 내 일상으로
에너지도 솔찮게 얻고 있다

아침 해 뜰 때까지 컴 끼고 앉아
직장 출근 안 하니까 왼 종일
도대체 밤낮도 없고
남들 눈치도 보지 않고
아예 나만의 방식 대로 한다
있는 에너지 다 소모시키면서
는적댈 새도 없이 나간다
여태 쓴 글은 수없이 많지만
인간이 덜 된 사람 같다

Acrostic

Actually

Basically good

Clean in metaphorically

Definitely fill me up

Even though stately friend

Friend of the friends

Get along if with you

However more funny world

I'm feeling be proud

Just learn a lesson in a subtly

Know my life flows into acrostic

Lot rewarding by good starting

Maybe I can't decide the last day

Now look forward you even today

- Korean Sonnet #118 / 2024. 4. 11

참 좋은 벗 - 행시(行詩)

참

좋은

은유로

나를 채울

의젓한 친구

벗 중에 벗이여

그대와 함께 하면

이 세상 더욱 즐겁고

름름해 지는 느낌이오

은연중에 교훈도 얻으니

행시 속으로 인생이 흐르고

시작이 좋아서 보람 또한 크며

라스트를 내가 정할 수는 없지만

오늘도 그대를 기다리고 있습니다

My Autumn Leaves

My articles such as these
You know write quick it, but

Actually my age already
Under the late fall in my life
Thinking back to the past now
Usually I'd accelerated at that time
Make another exciting event
Now and then that was erotic time

Leaves changed to white color
Emaciated my face nowadays
And lose weight of the body
Valuable living changed other
Eventually turn ugly to look at
So I'm thin looks like now

- Korean Sonnet #119 / 2024. 4. 11

나의 가을 단풍잎

지금 같은 글
금방 쓰지만

내 나이 벌써
인생 만추를 맞아
생각해 보면

가속하면서
을밋함 잊은 그땐
에로틱했지

단물 빠지고
풍채 초췌해 지니
잎사귀 말라

붉은 기운도
을씨년스레 변해
까칠해 지네

It is now or never

It is now you just do it
There is not soon enough
It's done, you try it
So just keep going like this

Not enough but it must be
Of course if you and I do it
Want it you can have indulgence

O.K. you never say "No"
Really have to be done

Now try it follow me
Even if it's difficult but start boldly
Very big goal if you have
Eventually it's nothing impossible
Really have to be done

- Korean Sonnet #122 / 2024. 4. 11

지금 아니면 안 돼

지금 그냥 하세요
금방은 아니어도
해보면 다 됩니다
요렇게 쭉 해봐요

아쉬워도 하세요
니캉 내캉 한다면
면죄부도 받아요

안 된다곤 마세요
돼야 하고 말고요

절 따라 해보세요
대범하게 시작해
로망 크게 가지면
안 되는 건 없어요
돼야 하고 말고요

How have you been

With fine rain, drizzle and misty rain
And hail and showers too
You know maybe the motivation is

Clear motion in la cumparsita-style
Untiring the law of inertia
Tightening of the perineum muscles

Action and reaction to almost death
Not ejaculate long hours to morning
Day by day enjoying the knowhow

Charming companions in my life
Let spend with my life's afternoon
Everyone who breathes inside of me
Anyway where are you like blue bird?
Really How have you been today?

- Korean Sonnet #126 / 2024. 4. 14

안녕하세요?

가랑비 안개비 보슬비에
나중에는 우박에 소낙비까지
다양한 원동력은 알다시피 아마도

라쿰파르시타풍(風)의 분명한 동작
마지막에 지치지 않는 관성의 법칙
바짝바짝 죄어주는 회음근의 탄력

사경에 이르는 작용과 반작용 법칙
아침까지 긴 시간 사출하지 않고
자제하고 날마다 즐기는 노하우

차밍한 내 인생의 동반자
카랑카랑한 내 삶의 오후를 함께 할
타인이면서 내 속에서 숨 쉬는 사람
파랑새 같은 그대, 어디 계신가요?
하우 헤브 유 빈 투데이 안녕하세요?

Flowers Enjoying

Abundant every branch

Be mild

Charming dahlia

Dazzle lilac

Elegant marronnier

Flowers just below

Good company

However

In there

Just take a seat

Knock to the carnation

Let see a soothingly

May be a surfboard riding

Now enjoying each other

- Korean Sonnet #129 / 2024. 4. 18

꽃들이 즐긴다

가지마다
나긋나긋
다알리아
라일락이
마로니에
바로밑에
사이좋게
아자아자
자리하나
차지하고
카네이션
타이르듯
파도타기
하고있네

Passionate Love

Probably a cup of **Jinro** <u>soju</u>

Almost become a drunkard

<u>**S**oju</u> **Like First Time** just a cup

Such as palatable as Rum, so

I melt the soul and then

Only dreaming of a long run

Now I'm living just my life

Actually I've been in love

Then I'd a lot of rendezvous

Eventually my normal life

Let's go to run without avoid

Only writing is my life first

Variably change litmus if it

Even I'll leave thinking it's last

- Korean Sonnet #130 / 2024. 4. 20

열애 (熱愛)

진로 한잔에
주태백 되고
처음처럼 한잔은
럼주처럼 입에 맞아
영혼을 녹여 담고
롱런을 꿈꾸며
한 생을 살아간다

사랑도 해봤고
랑데부도 많이 했지만
을밋한 내 인생

피하지 않고 달리겠다
우선 글만 쓰는 내 삶
리트머스가 변화하면
라스트로 알고 가겠다

You only it known

You know only yourself
Of course roman is good but
Usually now is the best time

Only you don't weigh merit and flaw
Now you'd better take carefree life
Let go of your ego too
You know on the proper line

I suggest open your wallet often
Thou when money blinds

Killing me only myself no choice
Now you'd better training for more
Of course to live with less money
What a more convenient to know
Now the last was not far away

- Korean Sonnet #145 / 2024. 5. 8

자신만 안다

꼼 **오**직 자신만 알고 있다
로망도 좋지만
지금이 제일 좋은 때다

唯 **유**불리 따지지 말고
유유자적 하라
자만심도 내려놓고
적당한 선에서

知 **지**갑도 가끔 열어라
금전에 눈이 멀면

足 **족**히 나 자신만 다쳐
한참 더 수양하고
줄여서 사는 것도
알아야 더 편리하다
라스트는 멀지 않았다

A Small Bird

A small cloud in the still night sky
Blind in the strange wind
Calming staying at there

A bird the size of chestnut
Busily search for the only house
Coming the world is always fast
Daylight is start finally but

Anyway little bird flies high in the sky
But still looking for a home
Could be long way from here
Dashingly flying on a daily

Actually the sky is wide and high
Based not easy to find my home but
Comfortable he find the place to rest

- Korean Sonnet #150 / 2024. 5. 14

김정호의 작은 새

고요한 밤하늘 작은 구름 하나
요요한 바람결에 눈이 멀어
한참 잠잠히 머물고

밤송이 만한 새 한 마리
하나뿐인 집을 바삐 찾는다
늘 빠르게 세상은 다가오고
에둘러 햇빛이 밝아오지만

작은 새는 높은 하늘을 날며
은연중 아직도 집을 찾는다
구만리 머나먼 길에서도
름름하게 날마다 날아간다

하늘은 넓고 높아서
나의 집 찾기 쉽지 않지만
가뿐하게 쉴 집을 찾는다

1978년 제가 대위 때, 노량진 화생방연구소 근무 시절
김정호가 방위병으로 와서 복무했는데, 집에 연락하면
부인이 갖고 온 기타로 내무반에서 하얀나비도 불렀음

Ping-Pong

Anyway years go by

Basically a languid body

Colonel Jung, Daumsaedai

Day by day with a racket

Every day I'm preparing it

Fast swing

Golden forty something

However I'm not a 40s but

I've confidence and

Just growing little by little

Key service finesse and

Lots smashing technique

Mastering of it and then

Now a day goes by

- Korean Sonnet #156 / 2024. 5. 20

탁구

가는세월
나른한몸
다음세대
라켓하나
마련해서
바삐치네
사십대도
아니지만
자신감이
차차늘어
카트서브
타격요령
파악하니
하루가네

It's me Seventies

I was born in 2. 21. 1951 lunar calendar

I'm a Jung, Dong-Hee, poet
The colonel retired from the army
So I write acrostic poem after retired
Mostly write bilingual acrostic with members
Everyday I live enjoy and pleasure

Seventy three years old from today
Eventually my info that's always open
Very busy life I've been, my evidence
Even almost all done to go end, I mean
Never want die middle of seventies
Ten year if more I live? I don't know
If I can live more three years from now
Eager acrostic book to give to the world
So I'll prepare it's the last chance to me

- Korean Sonnet #158 / 2024. 5. 21

六峰 鄭東熙 73세

육봉 정동희 시인입니다
봉직했던 육군에서 대령 전역
정년 퇴직 후 행시 쓰고 있지요
동호인들과 주로 영한대역 행시로
희희낙락 매일 즐겁게 삽니다

오늘부터 만 73세가 됐습니다
늘 오픈 돼 있는 제 회원 정보
부지런히 살았다는 증거이지요
터놓고 말해서 갈 날 다 됐지만
칠십대 중반에 죽고 싶지는 않고
십 년 정도 더 살 지는 모릅니다
삼 년 쯤만 내가 더 살 수 있어도
세상에 내놓고 싶은 행시집 몇 권
라스트라 생각하고 준비할 겁니다

MMXXIV ➔ LXXIII
2024년 ➔ 73세

실제보다 1년 3개월 늦은 오늘이, 호적상으로 제 생일입니다(1951. 음2. 21일생)

English Conversation

Anyway talk with American if possible

Basic point is **correct pronunciation**

Can't heard, if different pronounced

Definitely "Rion" and "Lion" are different

Even pronounce "end" as "don't block" or

Finally "By the way" as "Biden" if you talk

Graduate even if college, you can't heard

However kids don't learn grammar at first

If you saying, "End" to "Don't block"

Just learn by self, and then other sentence

Key cassette tapes also they don't listen

Language from other country also same

Maybe front of foreigners be discouraged

Now use even your **brave** gestures

- Korean Sonnet #159 / 2024. 5. 22

영어 회화

가능하면 미국인과 직접 대화하라
나의 기본 비결은 **정확한발음**이다
다르게 발음하면 못 알아 듣는다
라이온"과 "얼라이언"이 다르고
마지막"을 "막지마" 라고 발음하거나
바이더웨이"를 "바이든"으로 말하면
사년제 대학 나와도 못 알아듣는다
아이들은 처음부터 문법 안 배운다
자기 엄마 입을 보면서 따라 한다
차차 혼자 배우다가 다른 말도 배우고
카셋 테이프도 아이들은 안 듣는다
타국에서 건너 온 언어도 똑 같다
파란 눈 앞에 서면 기가 죽는데
하여튼 **용기 있게** *!!* 몸짓이라도 하라

Welcome to my world

Wonderful my world
English-Korean meaningful bilingual
Let's stay up all night in acrostic
Could be wriggling poetical idea
One world flinched
Moving with imagination
Ever a unique world

The full of romance
Old

Many exiting journey of writing
You know it with heavy rhyme

Wonderful fantasy world
On towards an eternal dream
Real like playing a concerto
Let's put the needs
Dreaming of the next generation

- Korean Sonnet #160 / 2024. 5. 25

환영합니다

나의 멋진 세상
의미 있는 영한대역

행시로 밤을 새자
시상이 꿈틀꿈틀

세상이 움찔움찔
상상으로 움직이는
으레 독특한 세상
로맨스로 가득한 곳

오래된
신나는 글의 여행

걸쭉한 운(韻) 넣고

환상의 세계
영원한 꿈을 향해
합주곡 연주하듯
니즈를 담아보자
다음 세대를 꿈꾸며

Star Young-Woong

Such a deep of the night
Though even in bright daylight
Anyway you are always my love
Really don't have to tell it

You are my shining love
Only my love
Usually even though comes fine rain
Now in the light of the stars
Go approaching like light to me

With if feel the same mind
Of course I'd like to meet quiet
Only with love mind
Not a rendezvous but even if
Going anyway, I'll come to you

- Korean Sonnet #165 / 2024. 6. 4

임영웅

밤 깊은 시간에도
하얗게 밝은 낮에도
늘 그대는 내 사랑
에둘러 말 안 해도

빛나는 그대 내 사랑
나만의 사랑
는개비가 와도
별빛을 받으며
빛처럼 다가오네

같은 마음이라면
은근히 만나고 싶어

사랑하는 마음으로
랑데부는 아니더라도
아무튼 간다 그대에게

Blood Donations

Because I'm too old, can't for it

Lots I had done it already

Of course because of my over age

Only I miss the past

Definitely there's still romance left

Donation blood timing was fixed

Of course when I was hot-blooded

Now I think it was great

Anyway didn't know about it till now

Text message received "Not allowed"

I knew that aren't possible things

On feel the limits of my abilities

Nowadays because I'm not chubby

So they asking me to pack a bag?

- Korean Sonnet #173 / 2024. 6. 8

헌혈 불가 통보

나이가 많다고 안 된대요
이미 많이 했다나요
초과된 나이 때문이래요
과거가 그립네요
로망은 분명히 남았는데

헌혈도 때가 있나 봐요
혈기 왕성했던 그때가
참 좋았단 생각이 드네요
여태 이런 건 몰랐는데
불가 통보 문자를 받았고
가능치 않은 일도 있구나
능력의 한계를 느낍니다
통통하게 살이 안 쪘다고
보따리 싸라는 건 아닌지

제목 : [혈액관리본부] 헌혈안내
[Web발신]
정동희님 그동안 헌혈참여에
감사드리며, 2017/05/21일
부터 연령초과로 헌혈참여가
불가능함을 알려드립니다. 늘
건강하시고 행복하세요.
♣헌혈고객지원센터

☎무료수신거부 080-800-3705

Fucks Your Minds

Finally never go to on strike hospital

Until closed never going there

Could be never go a strike hospital

King doctor for only patient

So lot of Korean people in ill humor

You'd better don't go bad hospital

Of course curse to bad hospital

Usually never go like that hospital

Real doctor who keep patient and heal

Mainly we want a good doctor

In doctor' heads be full of shit

Never we understand why do strike

Dear and kindly hospital only go

So never go to on strike hospital

- Korean Sonnet #177 / 2024. 6. 17

정신 나갔다, 병원 안 간다

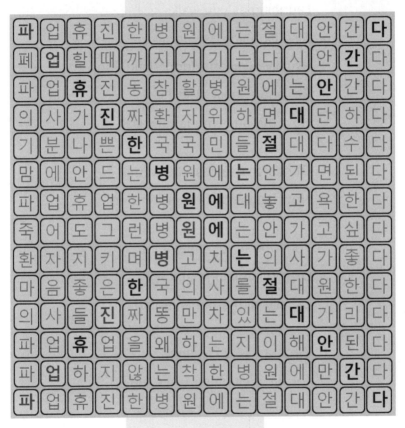

파 업 휴 진 한 병 원 에 는 절 대 안 간 **다**
폐 **업** 할 때 까 지 거 기 는 다 시 안 **간** 다
파 업 **휴** 진 동 참 할 병 원 에 는 **안** 간 다
의 사 가 **진** 짜 환 자 위 하 면 **대** 단 하 다
기 분 나 쁜 **한** 국 국 민 들 **절** 대 다 수 다
맘 에 안 드 는 **병** 원 에 **는** 안 가 면 된 다
파 업 휴 업 한 병 **원** **에** 대 놓 고 욕 한 다
죽 어 도 그 런 병 **원** **에** 는 안 가 고 싶 다
환 자 지 키 며 **병** 고 치 **는** 의 사 가 좋 다
마 음 좋 은 **한** 국 의 사 를 **절** 대 원 한 다
의 사 들 **진** 짜 똥 만 차 있 는 **대** 가 리 다
파 업 **휴** 업 을 왜 하 는 지 이 해 **안** 된 다
파 **업** 하 지 않 는 착 한 병 원 에 만 **간** 다
파 업 휴 진 한 병 원 에 는 절 대 안 간 **다**

105

Laugh on you want

Laughing as you walk

Also laughing as you go

Usually even after done laughing

Go laugh again at the last

How the one who laughs last

Of course he's just the winner

Now laughing with each other

You'd better to smile a lot

Or you laughing habitually

Usually with a big laughing

What a ka-ka-ka, laugh

Always if laughing while typing

Never old if you big laughing

Thou laugh! Ha-ha-ha

- Korean Sonnet #180 / 2024. 8. 6

웃어라

가면서도 웃고
나면서도 웃는다
다 웃고 나서
라스트에 또 웃자
마지막에 웃는 자가
바로 이기는 자다
사이 좋게 같이 웃고
아주 많이 웃으면 좋다
자꾸 습관적으로 웃거나
차이 나게 활짝 웃고
카카카 웃어 봐
타이핑 하면서도 늘 웃고
파안대소하면 젊어진다
하 하 하 웃어라

You Better Enjoy

You're if seventies

Of course, you're old enough

Usually after sleep, don't changed

Basically know it's not comfortable

Ever it's still middle-aged

Though it's not trying to your favor

That's what UN announcement says

Even it keeps increasing lifespan

Really do everything but play with fire

Enjoy what we've never done before

Now with optimism minds

Just take a look at it from now on

Only what can be doing naturally

You try all way to the last one

- Korean Sonnet #184 / 2024. 8. 10

인생 70 즐겨라

知 지금 당신이 70대라면
之 지긋한 나이지만
者 자고 나도 달라지지 않는다

不 불편한 곳도 있겠지만
如 여전히 중년이다
好 호감을 사려는 말이 아니고
之 지금 유엔 발표가 그렇다
者 자꾸 수명이 늘어난다고

不 불장난만 빼고 뭐든 해보자
如 여태껏 못해 본 걸 즐기자
樂 낙천적인 마음으로
之 지금부터라도 살펴보자
者 자연스럽게 할 수 있는 걸
라 라스트까지 한번 해보시라

공자님 말씀입니다. 知之者 不如好之者, 不如樂之者라
아는 者보다 좋아하는 者가 으뜸이고
좋아하는 者보다 즐기는 者가 으뜸이다

In My Old Age

Anyway in my old age

Be generous if you want to live it

Case by case keep in good standing

Day by day let's see right the world

Eventually if you don't keep in mind

Finally you become greatly regretted

Generally even if a universal terms

However you'd better think a greatful

I can't be born 12 times and

Just I can't die twice too

Keep the good things well if possible

Let's protect it

Maybe the life without a right answer

Now let's listen to it if it's real

- Korean Sonnet #187 / 2024. 8. 15

노후 처세 명심보감 12

노후를 맞아
후하게 살려면
처세를 잘 하고
세상을 바로 보자
명심하지 않으면
심하게 후회한다
보편적인 말이라도
감사하게 여겨라
열두 번 태어날 수 없고
두 번 죽을 수도 없다
가능하면 좋은 건 잘 유지하고
지켜 나가자
정답 없는 인생이지만
리얼하게 공감하면 새겨 듣자

1) 부르는 데가 있거든
   무조건 달려가라
2) 아내와 말싸움이 되거든
   무조건 져라
3) 일어설 수 있을 때
   무조건 걸어라
4) 남의 경조사에 나갈 때는
   제일 좋은 옷을 입고 나가라
5) 더 나이 먹기 전 아내가
   말리는 일 말고는 뭐든 해보라
6) 옷은 좋은 것부터 입고
   말은 좋은 말부터 하라
7) 누구든지 도움을 청하거든
   무조건 도와라
8) 안 좋은 일을 당했을 때는
   이만하면 다행으로 여겨라
9) 범사에 감사하며 살자
10) 나이 들어도 인기를 원한다면
    입은 닫고 지갑은 열어라
11) 보고 싶은 사람은 미루지 말고
    연락 해서 약속을 잡고 만나라
12) 어떤 경우에라도 즐겁게 살자

Alone

I am alone nowadays

I had my own parents

I had a big age difference brother but

I never had any sisters and

I don't have any cousins others have

I don't have any second cousins too

In my father is fourth only son, so

I didn't have any relatives as common

I had no choice but develop independence

I've solved everything on my own

I have a family and also a wife, but

I still take care of my bed and food alone

I guess I'm used to being alone

I guess I'll die while writing poem alone

- Korean Sonnet #188 / 2024. 8. 31

홀로

나는 요즘 혼자다
나름대로 부모님도 계셨고
나이 차이가 큰 형도 있었지만
나는 누나도 없고 여동생도 없었다
나는 남들 다 있는 사촌도 없고
나에겐 육촌도 없고 팔촌도 없다
나의 아버지께서 4대독자라서
나는 그 흔한 친척들도 없었다
나는 독립심을 키울 수밖에 없었고
나는 내 혼자서 모든 걸 해결해 왔다
나는 가족도 있고 마누라도 있지만
나는 지금도 혼자서 숙식을 해결한다
나는 혼자 지내는 게 익숙한 것 같다
나는 혼자 행시 쓰다가 죽을 것 같다

Better Everyday

Better day is coming
Even not the only me who knows
There's informed much subtly
Than daily with new eyes
Even fully worthy
Really diverse ideas

Even if the day changes
Valley that never dries up
Every day we meet again
Real new life opens up
You know it spreads to romance
Definitely without any interference
Anyway the trip out of the blue
Yeah, enjoy the next generation

- Korean Sonnet #189 / 2024. 9. 7

더 나은 매일

더 나은 날이 온다
나만 아는 게 아니고
은근히 정보가 많다
날마다 새로운 눈으로
온전히 가치 있는
다양한 아이디어

날이 새로 바뀌어도
마르지 않는 계곡
다시 맞이할 매일
새로운 삶이 열리고
로망으로 펼쳐진다
눈치 보지 않고
뜬금없는 여정
다음 세대를 즐긴다

Lotte Elite Team

let : actively cause something to happen
~에게 ~시키다, ~하게 해주다, 적극적으로 어떤 일이 일어나게 하다

> **L**otte Elite Team bravo
>
> **O**nly without damage let's go!
>
> **T**ake full accelerating
>
> **T**raining with good one
>
> **E**ven let's fulfill our dream

> **E**ven if insurance is difficult
>
> **L**et think it may be rough, but
>
> **I**f we've on the design well
>
> **T**he better result than planned
>
> **E**ven people change their lives

> **T**hou with lot a broad smile
>
> **E**ver with good match matching
>
> **A**fter a series of hits and
>
> **M**ay enjoy the next generation

- Korean Sonnet #191 / 2024. 9. 9

롯데 엘리트 팀

롯데 엘리트팀 만세
데미지 없다면 가자!
가속도 크게 붙이고
좋은 훈련 곁들여서
아롱진 꿈도 이루자

보험 일이 어려워도
험로일 순 있겠지만
설계만 확실히 하면
계획보다 좋은 결과
사람 인생을 바꾼다

활짝 많이 웃으면서
짝맞춤 착실히 해서
연거푸 히트 치면서
다음 세대를 즐겨요

Best Life Keeper

Basically with a calm heart
Even we've been having a nice chat
So I didn't do everything I wanted to do
Think I've been struggling all these years

Lot of things I've I couldn't quit
I've a wish cannot given up too
Finally we only pick what want to do or
Even we can't live without suffering

Keeping me before I get hurt and then
Even I want to live proudly once
Even if I live one day
Push off our laziness and
Eventually make my life better
Really want live once with confidence

- Korean Sonnet #192 / 2024. 9. 10

담담하고 단단하고 당당하게 살자

롯데손해보험 강사 허은영 AM 강의록 중에서

담담한 마음으로
담소만 그 동안 즐겼지만
하고 싶은 일 다 못 했고
고전만 그 동안 한 것 같다

단절하지 못한 것도 많고
단념할 수 없는 소망도 있다
하고 싶은 일만 골라 하거나
고생을 안 하고 살 수는 없다

당하기 전에 나를 지키고
당당하게 한번쯤 살고 싶다
하루를 살더라도
게으름 확 떨쳐버리고
살아온 인생 좀 더 바로 잡아
자신 있게 꼭 한번 살고 싶다

My First Payroll

My first payroll for insurance planner
You know above 8 million won without side leg

First month but it's a ton of money
I wish I could be like this every month
Really like it so much not add anything, so
Such as beyond what was received
To feel like my body is floating

Probably good started as insurance planner
Actually I met a strong force in a tough world
You know I need learn more insurance planning
Really need to come up with a new plan
Of course people saids no right answer to live
Lots experience with besides pay is needed
Long time I want to work here

- Korean Sonnet #193 / 2024. 9. 20

롯데손해보험 첫 급여

내가 받은 보험설계사 첫 급여
가지 떼고도 800만원 이상

첫 달인데도 엄청나게 많은 돈
달마다 이렇게 받으면 얼마나 좋을까
에누리 없이 진짜 너무 좋아서
받은 것 그 이상으로
은근히 몸이 붕 뜨는 기분이다

보험설계사 일은 잘 시작한 것 같다
험한 세상에 든든한 원군을 만났고
설계업무도 더 철저히 배워야 하고
계획도 정말 다시 세워야겠다
사람 사는 데 정답 없다고 하는데
급여 외에도 많은 경험 쌓으면서
여기서 오래 근무하고 싶다

Did you know what?

Day by day certainly become fades
It's because our life is so hard
Definitely increase hysteria

You have insurance?
Only to escape the harsh world
Usually you have to have insurance

Keep must be it
Now at a useful time
Of course not once, but many time
Without any damage, if to move on

What I think insurance is the best
How feel reassured even if times go
Anyway insurance that'll keep me strong
Take a look at it many ways

- Korean Sonnet #200 / 2024. 9. 21

보험을 아시나요?

확실성은 날로 옅어지고
실생활이 각박하다 보니
히스테리만 늘어난다

보험은 들고 계시죠?
험한 세상 피해 가시려면
은연중 꼭 들어야 해요

필히 지켜야 해요
요긴할 때 지금
한번이 아니라 여러번
데미지 없이 넘기려면

아무래도 보험이 최고죠
시간이 흘러도 든든한
나를 굳게 지켜줄 보험
요모조모 살펴보세요

Cancer Accident

Cancer or terrible disease are

Anyway implicitly approaching

Now comes like an accident

Caused by willful or not

Even it's hard to avoid an accident

Really even if have the same accident

Actually

Could be liable to a major breakdown

Could be cures a disease by doctor

In critical condition or dead, or

Disappointingly spend all There's fortune

Even can't be careful just you say

Now you should get insurance once

Thou let's work out better than anything

- Korean Sonnet #201 / 2024. 9. 22

암은 사고처럼 온다

암이나 무서운 질병은
은연중에 접근하고

사고처럼 다가오는 거라서
고의든 아니든 간에
와닿는 사고를 피하긴 어렵고

같은 사고를 당하더라도
다 같지는 않고
고장이 크게 날 수도 있다

의사가 병을 고쳐줄 수 있지만
사망 또는 중태에 빠지거나
가산을 다 탕진하기도 한다

말로만 조심한다고 안 된다
한번쯤 보험도 제대로 들고
다른 것보다 운동도 잘 하자

Out of insurance

Only dangerous and terrible things
Usually meet often a rough world
There is not stop at once or twice

Of course throughout my life
Finally I can't live with what I think

Insurance, especially non-life insurance
Now it'll guarantee a life without power
So whether it works or not
Usually you'll see if you look at it calmly
Really with accumulated experience and knowledge
Actually benefit and convenience of customers
Now insurance planner takes good care of you
Could be for your better life
Eventually trying to the last

- Korean Sonnet #202 / 2024. 9. 23

보험 없으면 위험한 인생

위험하고 끔찍한 일은
험한 세상에서 자주 만난다
한두 번으로 그치지 않는다

인생을 살아가면서
생각대로는 못 산다

보험, 특히 손해보험은
험 없는 삶을 보장한다
과연 효과가 있는지는
담담히 살펴보면 안다
쌓인 경험과 지식으로
고객의 이익과 편익을
살갑게 챙겨주는 설계사
더 나은 인생을 위해서
라스트까지 애를 쓴다

나의 Korean Sonnet
(英韓대역 14行詩)

2024년 10월 28일 발행

저　　자　정 동 희 (롯데손해보험 Life Planner)
이 메 일　daumsaedai@hanmail.net

편　　집　정 동 희
발　　행　도서출판 한행문학
등　　록　관악바 00017 (2010.5.25)
주　　소　서울시 중구 을지로 18길12
전　　화　02-730-7673 / 010-6309-2050
카　　페　http://cafe.daum.net/3LinePoem

정　　가　12,000원
I S B N　978-89-97952-58-8-04810

공급처　도서출판 한행문학 www.thankyouhangul.com
전　　화　010-6309-2050